AND THE FUTURE OF DARKNESS

Bath · New York · Singapore · Hong Kong · Cologne · Delhi · Melbourne

Written by Zed Storm
Creative concept and story by E. Hawken
Words by Rachel Elliot
Check out the website at www.will-solvit.com

First edition published by Parragon in 2010

Parragon
Queen Street House
4 Queen Street
Bath BA1 1HE, UK

ISBN 978-1-4454-0462-2

Printed in China

Please retain this information for future reference.

CONTENTS

Help!

CHAPTER ONE
PREDICTING THE FUTURE

"What a brilliant school project!" said my best friend Zoe.

She flipped an ollie and grinned at me. We had raced to the skate park after school. Normally school was the last thing we wanted to talk about when we were skating, but this project sounded awesome. We had to write about something that we hoped would be invented one day.

"Maybe Mrs Jones thinks one of us is going to be a great inventor, like my dad," I suggested.

"You probably are!" said Zoe. "I mean, you've got a time machine – all you have to do is visit the future and write about something you see there!"

Does that sound crazy? I should probably explain. I'm Will Solvit, and I'm an Adventurer, just like all my Solvit ancestors. My dad invented a fantastic machine that could become anything you needed. And after my parents went missing in a prehistoric jungle, what I needed was a time machine.

"There's no point in me trying to use Morph to visit the future for that," I said. (Morph can be kind of temperamental and the only way I can time travel is if there's an Adventure waiting for me!) "Besides," I added, "I've thought of a mega-cool idea for the project."

I did a 360 shoveit kickflip, whizzed around the skate park a couple of times and then flipped the board into my hands and gave a deep bow.

"So what's your mega-cool idea?" Zoe asked, rolling her eyes at me.

"Wait and see," I said. "We have to present the projects to the class tomorrow, right?"

"OK," said Zoe with a laugh. "But there's no way your idea's going to beat mine! What I've come up with is awesome!"

Name: Zoe
Project Title: The Earth Recycling Centre
Summary: My invention of the future is to turn our planet into a giant recycling centre!
How It Works: Every house on the planet has a trash chute in the kitchen. You just drop your trash into it and it gets sorted by an auto-recognition device. Then it falls into the recycling centre and gets recycled.

The auto-recognition device is able to automatically sort all your recycling so that you don't have to do a thing!

Benefits:

- All the things that people throw away appear on the other side of the world as brand-new goods.
- We no longer have to keep making new stuff, and that is great news for the environment.
- No more landfill!
- No more trash collections!

Potential Users: Everyone in the world!

Zoe did a mega-cool presentation, with tons of illustrations and a papier mâché model of the Earth Recycling Centre. The whole class thought it was the best idea so far... but they hadn't heard mine yet!

Name: Will

Project Title: Alien Defence Unit

Summary: The A.D.U. is a space patrol unit that roams around the Earth's atmosphere, capturing any aliens who want to attack us.

How It Works: The members of A.D.U. are highly trained super-cops for the space age! They have mega-fast spaceships, advanced technology and computers that can identify every known species in the galaxy.

The gadgets that the A.D.U. invents and uses will blow the minds of ordinary crime-prevention units!

The A.D.U. has links with all crime-prevention agencies across the galaxy, so they get the latest updates on wanted space criminals.

Awesome idea!

11

The A.D.U. Satellite Detention Centre is a secure unit to hold every kind of alien until they are brought to trial.

Only the very best candidates will be considered for the A.D.U., and they'll have to pass super-tough tests to get in. They won't be connected with any particular country – they'll represent the whole planet!

Benefits:

- Reduction of crime across the galaxy.
- Protecting Earth.
- Passing new technology to crime-prevention agencies on Earth.
- Improving Earth's relationship with other planets by helping them to reduce crime.

Potential Users: Everyone in the galaxy will benefit from the creation of the A.D.U.!

Giving my presentation was one of the coolest moments of my whole time at school so far! I handed round the prototype A.D.U. uniform I'd designed, and gave everyone in the class an A.D.U. badge.

Mrs Jones, our teacher, was so impressed with our presentations that she almost cracked a smile.

"Everyone has done an excellent job," she said. "I'm particularly pleased with Zoe and Will. Your presentations involved the whole class! I'm awarding each of you an A plus."

I couldn't believe it! Getting an A plus was about as normal for me as going to school on an elephant.

"Coming to hang out at mine to celebrate?" I asked Zoe as we headed out of school that afternoon.

"Sounds good," said Zoe, grinning at me.

We climbed into the car driven by my grandpa's chauffeur, Stanley. You see, I've been living at Grandpa Monty's house since Mum and Dad disappeared. Grandpa knows all about Adventuring because he was an Adventurer, too, and his special skill was spying. I can't wait to find out what my special skill is!

"Hi Stanley!" I said.

Stanley just raised one eyebrow about half a millimetre and drove smoothly off.

You might not think so to look at him, but Stanley's mega-cool. He's been Grandpa's chauffeur and odd-job man for as long as I can remember. He's really tall and thin and hardly ever says a word. He used to work for the President!

"So which of our inventions do you reckon will

come true first?" asked Zoe, bouncing up and down on the super-bouncy seat of Grandpa's car.

"Mine, got to be," I said.

"No way," Zoe replied. "The Earth Recycling Centre is just around the corner!"

"Want to bet?" I asked as the car rolled up Grandpa's drive towards Solvit Hall.

"Not on that," said Zoe, staring out of the window. "But I'll bet that you're going to get another one of those weird letters really soon."

I stared at her. I always knew when an Adventure was about to start because a letter would turn up to point me in the right direction. Trouble was, I had no idea who was sending the letters or when the next one would arrive.

"What do you mean?" I asked. "How could you know that?"

Zoe burst into laughter and pointed out the

window. I couldn't believe my eyes!

"Awesome!" I yelled.

The car pulled up and we jumped out and raced over to the front door. A familiar white envelope was pinned to the dark wood! I tore it down and ripped it open. My heart was hammering with excitement.

WHAT DO YOU CALL A SPACESHIP WITH A FAULTY AIR-CONDITIONING UNIT?

A FRYING SAUCER!

YOUR IDEA FOR THE A.D.U. WAS AWESOME, BUT NOW YOU'RE ABOUT TO PROTECT THE WORLD FOR REAL! IT'S ALMOST TIME FOR ANOTHER ADVENTURE. GET READY FOR A JOURNEY INTO THE FUTURE.

YOU'LL SOON BE DEFENDING THE PLANET, JUST LIKE THE A.D.U.

GOOD LUCK, WILL!

"A toast to the future!" Grandpa Monty exclaimed.

We each raised a sparkling glass of pop and clinked glasses. Grandpa had decided to cook up a feast to celebrate our project grades. I'm pretty used to Grandpa's weird taste in food, but Zoe went kind of green when she tried the eel cake.

"I really like these pickle-and-strawberry sandwiches, Grandpa!" I said, distracting him so that Zoe could spit her mouthful of eel cake into a paper towel.

"Me too, Henry, me too," said Grandpa. (He hardly ever gets my name right!) "Have you tried the tuna-and-carrot toffee?"

Ugh!

17

"Derishush," I said through a mouthful of the toffee.

It was an awesome feast. I avoided anything that had kippers in it (scones and olives), but I stuffed my face with everything else.

"You're not going to be able to fit into Morph after that lot," said Zoe.

I leaned back in my chair and patted my bulging waistline.

"No point starting an Adventure on an empty stomach!" I told her.

"Adventure?" said Grandpa Monty. "But you've only just come back from the last one!"

"That was weeks ago, Grandpa!" I exclaimed. "Anyway, it's not as if I can do anything about it – once Adventures start happening, they just seem to keep on happening."

"You're far too excitable, young Henry," said

Grandpa. "Have some eel juice."

"I'm Will, Grandpa," I said automatically. "Er, I think I'll pass on the eel juice, thanks. I've got to get ready for my Adventure."

Two chairs scraped on the tiled floor as Zoe and I stood up at the same time.

"Thanks for the feast, Mr Solvit," she said. "I've never seen anyone make profiteroles like that before."

"The secret's in the liver pâté, young lady," said Grandpa, tapping his finger on the side of his nose.

"Let's go," I broke in before Zoe could start going green again.

We raced up the spiral staircase that led to my bedroom. I couldn't wait to get started! I burst into my room, grabbed my backpack and cranked my brain into gear to think about what I'd need on this trip. I had brought a whole load of Dad's awesome inventions with me to Solvit Hall, and they had already saved my life several times on Adventures!

"Stun gun?" I muttered to myself. "Maybe. Will it work on aliens though? Truth serum – yeah – might come in handy."

"Will, you know it's the first sign of madness to start talking to yourself, don't you?" Zoe enquired, handing me the pen that can write in any language.

"You know what the second sign of madness is?" I asked her.

"What?"

"Hanging out with someone who talks to himself," I replied.

"You're so sharp you might cut yourself," said Zoe with deep sarcasm. "Listen, Time Boy, I reckon you might need some help on this Adventure."

"What sort of help?" I asked.

"My sort of help," said Zoe. "I was useful when you were fighting Dr Demonax, wasn't I?"

"Yes," I agreed. "But what makes you think I'll need you so much on this Adventure?"

"It's not you, it's the planet that needs me!" said Zoe, flailing out her arm in a grand sweeping gesture. "I want to find a scientist to help me with my recycling idea."

"You mean...a scientist from the future?"

"Top marks, Einstein!" she joked. "Oh come on, Will, please say yes! I really want to find out if my invention has a chance of coming true."

Her eyes were pleading. I thought about all the

times she had helped me out. If it hadn't been for her, I might be penguin food. Plus, I kind of liked the idea of having some company this time.

"OK," I said. "You can come – as long as you promise that you won't get in the way of the Adventure."

Zoe held her hand up beside her head in a sort of salute.

"I promise, Captain," she said, trying to hide a smile.

"Right, you can help me pack the Adventure kit," I said.

Zoe is way more organized than me and she had soon stocked my backpack with everything we thought we might need. Our kit included:

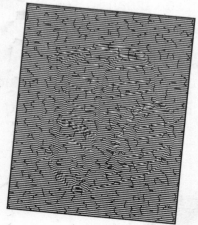

- Stun gun
- Truth serum
- Uncuttable rope
- Pen that can write in any language
- Camouflage paint
- Grandpa's spy diary
- Morph's memory chips
- Memory obliterator
- Night-vision goggles
- Omnilume

Finally, I remembered to put my SurfM8 internet phone into my pocket. Zoe had her SurfM8 with her too. I didn't intend for us to get separated, but you never know what might happen on an Adventure, and it's worth having some way to communicate!

I fired up Morph and stepped inside, followed

by Zoe. Just then, my bedroom door burst open and Grandpa's dog Plato rocketed into Morph!

"Everyone wants to go on this Adventure!" I exclaimed. "Have you got an invention to check out in the future too, Plato?"

"Remote-controlled dog-flaps?" Zoe suggested, closing Morph's door.

"Nah, automatic cat-catchers!" I said, rubbing Plato's back. "OK, everyone, here we go. Hold on tight!"

Morph usually rattled, shook and bumped while time travelling – it was kind of like rolling down a hill inside a washing machine. But this time was different. My stomach didn't churn and my legs didn't shake. The only thing that happened was that my head felt as if it was spinning on my neck!

"Ugh, I feel really dizzy," said Zoe.

She reached out a hand to steady herself
against the wall, missed and staggered sideways.
I grabbed her as Plato collapsed onto the floor.

"I think my eyes are falling out of my head," I
said, rubbing them. "That was the weirdest trip
I've ever had in Morph!"

"Come on," said Zoe. "Let's see where we
are!"

She flung open the door and her shoulders
sagged.

"It hasn't worked," she said, sounding really
disappointed.

I followed her out and found that we were still
in my bedroom. Plato trotted out too, and Morph
immediately shrank down to miniature size.

"No, Morph!" I yelled.

But the time machine took no notice – it didn't
want to travel any further. I shoved Morph into

my pocket and Zoe groaned.

"That's so annoying!" she said. "Now what?"

I didn't reply. I was too busy staring around the room. Something was wrong. It was definitely my room – all my furniture was there – but someone had taken all my stuff.

"Will?" said Zoe. "Earth to Will!"

"There's something funny going on," I said, looking around. "Just look...there should be piles of comics on that desk, and my homework..."

"And that mound of stinky clothes in the corner," Zoe added. "Maybe your grandpa's been tidying up."

"What, in the last two minutes?" I asked. "I don't think so. Besides, he wouldn't go near my stinky clothes."

"No one would without a face mask," Zoe pointed out.

I was saved from having to think up a brilliant comeback by the sight of a white envelope on the bedroom floor.

PATIENT: "DOCTOR, DOCTOR, I KEEP SEEING INTO THE FUTURE!"

DOCTOR: "WHEN DID THIS START?"

PATIENT: "NEXT TUESDAY AFTERNOON."

CHILL OUT, WILL, MORPH HASN'T MADE A MISTAKE. WELCOME TO ONE OF THE BIGGEST DAYS OF YOUR LIFE. YOU'RE ABOUT TO FIND OUT WHO YOU REALLY ARE. TAKE A DEEP BREATH AND WALK OUT OF YOUR BEDROOM.

HAVE FUN!

I shoved the letter into my pocket and strode over to my bedroom door.

"Come on, let's explore," I said.

We walked out onto the landing. It was really quiet. I couldn't hear the usual sounds of Grandpa Monty experimenting in the kitchen, and there were no weird kipper smells drifting up the spiral staircase. The whole place made me feel as if I should walk around on tiptoe. I peered down into the hallway. I could see Grandpa's wooden hat stand, but it was in a different place from normal, and there was a mirror that I didn't recognize.

"Check this out!" said Zoe in a hissing whisper. She was looking up at the portraits of my Solvit ancestors, which had been hanging on the wall there for as long as I could remember.

"Forget them," I whispered. "That's the past – we want the future."

"Seriously," said Zoe. "Look at this."

Even in a whisper I could tell that she wasn't going to let this go. I peered up at the portrait she was pointing at...and then I felt my knees go weak.

It was a portrait of me!

← Handsome, eh? :)

Underneath the picture was a small brass plaque with words engraved on it.

WILL SOLVIT
Time Traveller

I thought my head was going to start spinning again. Ever since I found out that I was an Adventurer I had been wondering what my special skill was. At last I had found out!

"Close your mouth, you look like a goldfish," said Zoe. "How come you're looking as if I've just hit you with a brick?"

"I'm...I'm a time traveller!" I said, turning to look at her. "That's my special skill!"

"No kidding, Sherlock," she replied in a dry voice. "Well, it was never going to be detective work, was it?"

"What do you mean?" I asked.

"I mean that you've been time travelling all along, through all your Adventures," Zoe replied. "It doesn't take a genius to figure out that you're – oh no! Someone's coming!"

The front door had burst open – there was no time to run. Besides, my legs felt as if they had turned to lead. A man strode in with three kids behind him. He looked up and saw us staring down at him from the landing.

"Now we're in trouble," said Zoe under her breath.

"Will Solvit!" the man yelled.

He didn't sound angry. In fact, he sounded mega-excited. He ran up the spiral staircase and gave me a big hug. Then he shook Zoe's hand and petted Plato. Grandpa's dog backed away behind my legs, looking alarmed.

"You all look so shocked!" he said with a laugh. "OK, let's take it from the top. I'm Jon, and those are my kids – Sarah, Mandy and Jamie."

I looked down at the three kids in the hallway. They all grinned up at me and waved.

"Are you...a Solvit?" I asked, trying to jump-start my brain. "I mean – I guess this is the future, right?"

"Spot on," he told me. "No, I'm not a Solvit, but they are. I married Jenny Solvit, you see."

"Who's that?" asked Zoe.

"She's a fantastic Adventurer," said Jon with pride ringing in his voice. "She's also Will's great-great-granddaughter."

"No way," said Zoe.

"Now who looks like a goldfish?" I murmured.

It was funny, but I didn't feel at all freaked out by meeting my descendants. I had met quite a few of my ancestors when I travelled into the past – this was no different, really. It was pretty cool to see my great-great-great-grandchildren though!

"Jenny's away on an Adventure right now," said Jon. "She'll be gutted that she missed you."

"What's her special skill?" I asked.

"Invisibility," Jon replied.

"Awesome," said Zoe and I together.

"Come down and meet the kids," Jon suggested. "I'll dig out something to eat and we can all have a good talk."

He led us downstairs, where my three great-great-great-grandchildren were kicking off their trainers.

"Say hi to Will," their dad told them.

The two girls smiled at me, but Jamie bounded up and shook my hand. He looked about a year younger than me, and his eyes were sparkling with excitement.

"It is so bad to meet you," he gasped.

I must have looked as blank as I felt, cuz Jon laughed and ruffled Jamie's hair.

"He means it's really cool to meet you," Jon explained. "Don't worry, Will, I don't get modern kid-speak either!"

Now that made me feel weird! Suddenly I knew how my teachers feel when we talk about stuff they don't understand. What else was I going to find bizarre about the future?

"Sorry, I'll try to remember," said Jamie. "It's just so crank to meet you! I can't wait to start Adventuring. It'll be mega."

He said 'crank' and 'mega' in the same way that I'd say 'awesome' or 'cool'. Mandy and Sarah were giggling now. Jamie scowled at them.

"Ignore my idiot sisters," he said. "They don't want to be Adventurers. All they care about is downloading the latest celeb gossip and chatting on the holophone to their stupid boyfriends. Boring!"

"Just cuz we don't spend our whole time reading about the past, he thinks we're boring!" said Sarah.

"OK, OK, let's not have a row in front of Will," said Jon. "Come on, gang, let's hit the kitchen and find some food."

Suddenly a loud, vibrating ring echoed through the house.

"The holophone!" squealed Sarah.

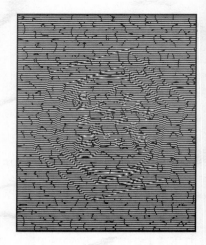

"It'll be Zack for me!" Mandy cried.

They raced into the sitting room and Jamie rolled his eyes at me.

"See!" he said.

We went into the kitchen and I stopped dead in my tracks. Plato walked into me and gave a woof of complaint.

"This is awesome!" I said.

The kitchen looked completely different from how it did in my time. It was gleaming and shiny, with no biscuit tins, tea bags or recipe books cluttering up the surfaces. In fact, it looked as if no one had ever cooked in there at all.

Jon pressed his hand against a shiny red door. It lit up in the shape of his hand.

"Hi, Jon," said an electronic voice. "What can I get for you?"

"Snacks and drinks for Jamie, two guests and me, please," said Jon.

There was a sort of muted whirring sound – like a computer hard drive firing up. Then a square hole opened in the middle of the big kitchen table, and a tray rose out of it filled with steaming hot drinks, crisps and samosas with dip.

"Woah," I said, pulling up a chair and taking the mug that Jon handed to me. "I wish this kitchen existed in my time!"

I sipped the drink. It was frothy hot chocolate, and it tasted as if someone had filled a mug with

Yum yum!

37

hot water and then dipped a bar of chocolate in it for about ten seconds.

"Will, check this out!" said Jamie, pulling something out of a big cupboard in the corner. "Everyone knows that you really love skating!"

"A skateboard!" I exclaimed, and then noticed that its wheels were missing. "Oh, it's broken."

"No it's not!" he said, laughing. "Look..."

He let go of the board, but instead of clattering to the floor it just floated in the air, about fifteen centimetres off the ground. I was almost drooling – it was a hoverboard!

"Wicked!" I whispered, feeling kind of awed. "I've read about people trying to make these... How fast can it go?"

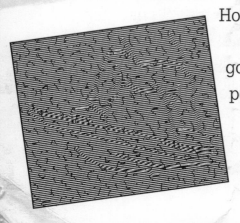

"You're not supposed to go more than fifteen miles per hour," said Jamie, "but I've been tinkering with this one and I can get her up to twenty-five."

"Her?" Zoe repeated, looking disgusted. "Oh pur-lease. Can we cut the skater-waffle? I want to know where I can find the nearest scientist."

Jon and Jamie looked puzzled, so we explained Zoe's idea to them.

"Nothing like that's been invented yet," said Jon. "But I do know a few scientist types who might be able to help."

"That's great!" said Zoe, standing up. "Let's go!"

"Go where?" Jon enquired.

"To find your scientist friends, of course. That's why I'm here!"

Zoe was trying really hard to be polite. She can be really single-minded though. When she gets her teeth into an idea, pulling her away from it is like trying to take a human girl from a hungry T-rex (and I should know).

"But you can't see them now," said Jon, looking very surprised. "It'll be weeks before we come out of hiding. I thought you had come here to help us!"

"We don't know why we came here yet," I said, frowning at Zoe. "What do you mean about being in hiding?"

"We only came back here to pack our bags," said Jon.

"But why?" I asked.

Jamie looked at me in surprise.

"Don't you know?" he asked in astonishment. "It's the Darkness, Will. The Darkness is coming!"

CHAPTER FOUR
THE FLYING CAR

I really didn't like the sound of that. I hadn't got a clue what the Darkness was, but sometimes you just know when something isn't good.

"I almost forgot about it in the excitement of meeting you," said Jon. "But we have to hurry."

He strode out of the kitchen and I quickly followed him.

"What's the Darkness?" I asked. "Why is it out to get you? Can I help?"

"It's not just us – it's the whole planet," said Jon. "Seriously, we have got to get a move on. I'll explain everything when we're safely in hiding, but right now..."

"We're here to help," I said. "Zoe can give the girls a hand with their packing and I'll help Jamie."

I raced upstairs with Jamie. He had the room that Stanley sleeps in now! He pulled a metallic-coloured backpack from under his bed and started shoving stuff into it. I saw him pack a mega-weird pair of sunglasses, a computer tablet and a handheld gaming device. He looked as though he had a whole Adventure kit in his backpack already! He waved his hand over the top of the bag and it sealed itself.

"I thought your dad said you'd be away for weeks?" I asked.

"Probably," said Jamie, sounding a bit dismal.

"Shouldn't you be packing some clothes then?" I reminded him.

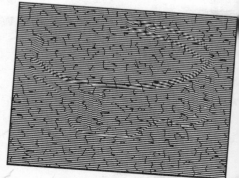

He was wearing a pair of blue jeans and a white T-shirt. He stared at me in confusion, and then grinned.

"Watch this," he said, putting his backpack down.

He reached around to the label inside his T-shirt collar, and I saw that there was a tiny button on it. He pressed it and spoke in a loud voice.

"Requesting a fresh change of clothes," he said.

There was a sort of shimmer and suddenly he was wearing brown combats and a green T-shirt. My chin nearly hit the floor!

"That is totally awesome!" I stated.

"Everyone just has one suit," Jamie explained, shouldering his backpack again. "It can change into anything you want. Luckily they've added voice-recognition software to them now. My sisters used to think it was hilarious to press the label button and change my jeans into a dress or something."

"Wow," I said. "I wish I had one of those! Stanley would never have to touch my stinky piles of clothes again!"

"I've heard of that!" said Jamie in great excitement. "It was called 'doing the laundry', wasn't it? Mental."

"But there must be something you have to wash nowadays?" I said.

"Nope," said Jamie as we walked downstairs. "Everything's made from the same technology – it just changes into whatever you want it to be."

"Like Morph," I said.

"Yeah," Jamie agreed, and I realized that he must know all about my time machine.

"Everything's powered by the same dark energy as Morph. Your dad was a total genius."

"Yeah," I said, wondering for the zillionth time where Dad was. Before Dad had gone missing, he'd harnessed dark energy (that's the energy in the universe that no one can really explain) to power Morph. Jamie was right, my dad was a genius.

On my Adventures I had collected a few clues about where my parents had gone after I lost them in the jungle. I had learned that:

1. I will find one parent before I find the other.
2. Neither of them is where I left them.
3. The Partek said that my dad is in a place where I will never find him, but as they are human-hating cat-shaped

aliens, I'm taking it with a pinch of salt.

4. Mum and Dad made a time machine that took them to the Stone Age.
5. Mum left Dad behind in the Stone Age and went off somewhere in the time machine.
6. Dad got into a Partek spaceship.
7. Mum is stuck somewhere between the Stone Age and the present.
8. I should look for Mum in the past.
9. I should look for Dad in the future.
10. Dad sent me a message that I am going to have to fight against a great evil. The battle will take place in outer space. I'll need the Aztec mask to defeat the evil.

Hopefully I'd find out more during my next Adventure...whatever it was. I couldn't wait to find out more about this Darkness.

When we got downstairs, Jon was waiting in the hallway with Mandy, Sarah, Zoe and Plato.

"Will!" Zoe exclaimed when she saw me. "They have got the most amazing clothes!"

"I know," I said. "I hope that invention happens in our lifetime!"

Mandy and Sarah were kneeling down beside Plato, patting and stroking him. He rolled over onto his back and closed his eyes in bliss.

"He's so gorgeous!" Sarah said. "You're so lucky to be able to have a pet!"

"Aren't you allowed to have one?" I asked in surprise.

Jon didn't seem like the kind of person who would stop his kids from having a pet. Actually he was pretty cool...for a dad.

"No one can have pets," Mandy explained. "It's too dangerous."

"Dangerous?" I repeated. "But Plato's not dangerous!"

"You don't understand," said Sarah, looking up at me with big, scared eyes. "The Partek can control any pet these days – not just cats. They've evolved since your time."

I exchanged a worried look with Zoe. If the Partek were involved, this Adventure had just become a whole new kind of dangerous. I opened my mouth to ask more, but Jon hustled us all out of the house.

"Come on, all of you, get a wriggle on."

"Will," said Zoe in a low voice as we stepped out of Solvit Hall. "How can the Partek be here? I thought you got rid of them?"

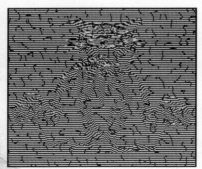 Way back when I was just starting to be an Adventurer, I came face to

whiskers with a mega-weird alien race called the Partek. They very nearly took over the world, but luckily Zoe and I were able to help out.

"I don't know," I whispered back. "But I've got a horrible feeling we're going to find out."

A very short time later we were flying through the clouds in Jon's dark-energy-powered car.

Now, I bet you've imagined flying cars. They're one of those inventions that everyone thinks will come along sooner or later. But let me tell you, nothing can prepare you for how mega-mega-cool they are! Jon's car was silver, sleek and long, with three rows of seats, drinks and snack machines and padded chairs that adjusted to the shape of each passenger's body.

It felt amazing to be soaring through the sky,

leaning back on a seat as soft as a cloud. I was in the front row, by the window. Zoe was between Jon and me, and Jamie was in the row behind us with his sisters. Plato was between Sarah and Mandy, loving the attention they were giving him. There were tons of other flying cars all around us, all full of scared-looking people.

"We have to sign in at the checkpoint," Jon explained. "Then we go into hiding underground."

The car slowed as we joined a queue. I couldn't get my head around the fact that we were just hovering there in a car!

"While we're waiting, can you explain about the Partek?" I asked Jon. "What's been going on?"

"Hang on a sec," said Jon, twisting around to look at his kids. "You three, it's time for your lesson. Glasses on."

Zoe and I turned to stare at the young Solvits behind us. Jamie opened his backpack and pulled out the weird sunglasses I'd seen earlier. They were slightly greenish, and made out of one curving piece of plastic. Mandy and Sarah had similar glasses, but Mandy's were red and Sarah's were blue.

"Dad, couldn't we miss school this once?" Jamie asked.

"No way," said Jon. "What would your mum say? Glasses on, you lot."

The three of them grimaced and put the glasses on. They each pressed a button on the side of the glasses and a couple of earplugs shot out and into their ears. I saw images start flickering across the insides of the glasses.

"That's school?" Zoe gasped. "Oh, I am loving

AWESOME!!!

the future!"

"It's a virtual classroom and they have a virtual teacher," said Jon as the car crept forward in the queue. "The different colours show which year they're in."

"Will, don't you think that sounds cool?" said Zoe.

"It just sounds like another lame try by the grown-ups to make school fun," I said, rolling my eyes at her. "You're way too keen on schoolwork, Zoe."

Jon gave a snort of laughter. "You sound just like Jamie," he said. "OK, so you want to know about the Partek."

"I knew we hadn't heard the last of them," I said, thinking of the last time I had seen the vicious cat people.

"They've been visiting Earth for years," Jon

said, sounding suddenly weary. "Every time they come, they bring so many spaceships that they block out the light from the sun. That's why we started calling it the Darkness."

"But why do they come?" I asked.

"For us," said Jon, staring straight ahead of him. "They come for the human race."

I felt as if cat claws were scratching the inside of my brain.

"I don't get it," said Zoe.

"He means that they come here to capture people," I told her. "Right, Jon?"

Zoe's hand crept up to cover her mouth.

"Right," said Jon.

"What for?" Zoe asked.

"No one knows," said Jon, turning to look at us. "Because no one ever comes back. Whatever the Partek do to them...it's forever."

CHAPTER FIVE
AN OLD ENEMY

"Everybody out," said Jon a short while later.

We had been queuing for ages. Jamie, Mandy and Sarah had finished their virtual class and were trying to get out of doing their virtual homework when we arrived at the floating car park.

"But how do we get out?" I asked, trying – and failing – to see the ground below us.

Jon just grinned at me and pressed a button on the dashboard.

"Engaging teleport," said an automated voice.

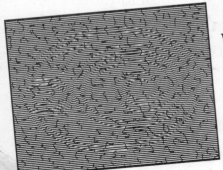
Suddenly everything went wobbly! It was like being trapped

inside a rainbow-coloured snow-shaker. I couldn't open my mouth or move my arms or legs. There was a high-pitched warbling ringing sound in my ears, and my vision was blurred. I really hoped I wasn't doing something embarrassing like fainting. Then I felt a blast of cold, fresh air and firm ground beneath my feet.

"I hate teleporting," said Sarah.

We were standing in a field beside a large hill. There was a big, oblong entrance cut into the side of the hill, and a stream of people was steadily pouring into it. Between the entrance and us were about ten checkpoints.

"We'll sign in and soon be safe inside," said Jon.

We joined a queue for one of the checkpoints. Sarah and Mandy started chatting about something totally girly and I zoned out.

I want one!

"Will, I brought my hoverboard," said Jamie. "You want to have a go?"

"Totally!" I said.

He dropped the board and I lifted one foot onto it, hopped up...and fell off. Jamie howled with laughter.

"Hey, there's Charlie Steelman!" said Jon, nudging Zoe. "He's a scientist – he might be just the person for you to talk to about your recycling idea."

Zoe was gone like a shot, and I fell off the hoverboard again.

"You have to think about your balance," hooted Jamie, wiping tears of laughter from his eyes.

I guess that was where I made my big mistake. After all, I knew that I was there for an Adventure. I knew what the Partek were like. I should have been staying alert, not mucking

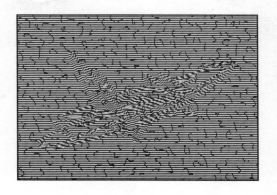

around on
Jamie's
hoverboard.
But it was
super-cool!

After about three more tries, I managed to get
up on the board without falling off. I could feel it
through my feet, kind of bobbing in the air. Now
I was on it, I realized that it was just the same as
a normal skateboard – it felt as if it was a part of
me in just the same way.

"I think I've got it!" I yelled in triumph.

Suddenly there was a WHUMP! Above our
heads a Partek space fleet was zooming towards
us. Everything went dark. The crowd around
us went into panic overdrive – everyone was
screaming and running in different directions –
we must have looked like ants to the Partek.

57

Inside its mouth were rows of needle-sharp teeth, and instead of a tongue it had a scaly arm coming out of its mouth, with deadly claws on the fingers.

"I have been looking forward to meeting you, Will Solvit," hissed the Partek.

He slinked closer, never moving directly towards us, but always drawing nearer.

"Let this boy go," I demanded. "You want me? Well, fine, you got me. You don't need him."

"On the contrary," said the Partek, with what sounded almost like a purr. "Two Solvits for the price of one. Quite a bargain."

The light grew brighter, and I saw that we were inside a sort of mini docking bay. We were surrounded by Partek.

"Let me introduce myself," said the Partek. "I am Captain Savage, of the glorious 14th Partek

Regiment. Oh, and I am now your owner!"

He scraped his claws along the metal floor of the spaceship and made my nerves jangle. Plato was pressed up against me, shaking like a jelly in a blender.

"We have captured you," said the Partek in a soft, sing-song voice. "That makes you...let me see...ah yes. That makes you our prisoners."

"Like father, like son," said a gravelly voice from the shadows.

"What's that supposed to mean?" I demanded.

No one answered. My thoughts rattled around in a panic. I knew that Dad had gone off with the Partek. Was he still with them?

Poor Plato!

"You don't scare us!" Jamie shouted.

He was a brave kid! At that moment I felt really proud that I was his ancestor.

"No?" whispered Captain Savage. His razor-filled smile widened. "But we will, child, we will. There's all the time in the world."

"Where are you taking us?" I asked.

"You should thank us, Will," he replied. "We're taking you home."

My mind boggled.

"You mean, you're taking me to the past?"

He made a weird sound – something between choking on a hairball and gurgling like a baby. I guessed it was supposed to be a laugh, but it didn't make me feel very cheerful.

"I'm taking you to the last home you will ever have," he stated with a cruel edge in his voice.

"You reckon?" I muttered under my breath.

"There is a planet far from here," Captain Savage said. "It is a beautiful, distant place. Its name is Clawmore."

"Wow, it sounds really welcoming," I said with sarcasm.

"Silence!" he shrieked. "Clawmore is your new home. I trust you will like it there, because you are never going to leave!"

"I defeated your lot once before, Furball," I shouted at the Partek. "I can do it again."

My enemy's whiskers twitched.

"Aw, am I getting to you?" I asked. "Shame."

Inside I felt as shaky as Plato, but I knew that I had to keep up a show of confidence. I couldn't let Jamie see how worried I was.

"That was a long time ago for us," he said, his lips curling. "We have learned much since then. But you are still just a boy. You cannot stop us."

"But what's in it for you?" I asked. "Why would you want to take us to live on some random planet?"

WILL'S FACT FILE

Dear Adventurer,

I bet this isn't the first story you've read about time travel. I expect you've read science-fiction books and seen lots of futuristic movies. But what do we really know about the future?

The answer is nothing for sure. OK, we might know that Grandma is coming to tea next Thursday, but what about 50 or 100 years from now? What will that be like? Only a real time traveller, like me, can know for sure. And I'm not going to spoil the surprise!

Check out the facts that we do know, and amaze your friends with your knowledge.

Time Travel

Time travel isn't possible in the real world but stories about time travellers have been around for centuries.

- Urashima Tarõ is an ancient Japanese legend about a fisherman who travels to the future.

- In 1819 Washington Irving published 'Rip Van Winkle', a short story about a man who falls asleep and wakes up 20 years in the future.

- Charles Dickens' 'A Christmas Carol', published in 1843, is a tale of an old miser who travels backwards and forwards in time.

- 'A Connecticut Yankee in King Arthur's Court' (1889) is Mark Twain's humorous adventure of an American travelling back in time to medieval England.

- H.G. Wells' story 'The Time Machine' (1895) was the first story to use a machine to travel through time.

DID YOU KNOW...

If time travel really was possible, there would be time travellers telling us about their adventures right NOW!

Looking Ahead

People have always been fascinated with the future and have tried to predict it in various ways.

- In ancient Greece oracles studied animals' insides to tell the future.

- Prophets (or seers) say they receive messages from supernatural beings about things that are going to happen.

- Leonardo da Vinci predicted the future through his drawings of robots, cars and flying machines.

- In the 16th century Nostradamus successfully predicted some major world-changing events.

- Fortune tellers use everything from crystal balls to tea leaves to predict what is going to happen, normally for a fee.

- Some psychics and mediums have premonitions — feelings and flashes about future events.

- Some people appear to be able to see into the future just because they have ideas ahead of their time.

- Futurologists use scientific information to predict trends.

DID YOU KNOW...

In the future there will probably be disease and pollution forecasts as well as weather forecasts.

Our changing world

The world's population is growing incredibly quickly.

- It is forecast that it will reach nine thousand million by 2050.
- More and more people will live to over 100.
- Fossil fuels (coal, oil and gas) will be a thing of the past.
- The sun, wind, rain and tides will be used to create energy.

We will have to grow more food to feed the growing population.

Our shrinking world

Technology is constantly evolving to make our world seem smaller.

- International trade means that many things are from distant places.
- By surfing the internet we can get information on just about anything.
- Videophones mean we can speak face-to-face with people far away.
- In the future nationalities and borders will become less obvious.

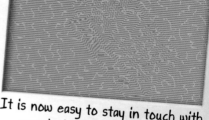

It is now easy to stay in touch with people in distant countries.

Towns

As our population grows, there will be purpose-built towns and cities.

- Buildings will need to withstand extreme weather.
- Most vehicles will have to travel below or above ground.
- There will be few shops because people will shop mostly online.
- Pavement escalators will hurry people along streets.

High-rise offices and flats will get taller and taller.

...mes of the future

...uturistic features are already working ...eir way into our homes.
Rainwater can be collected and used around the home.
Voice recognition lets you control a room's temperature with your voice.
Face recognition that may one day replace keys is being developed.
Talking mirrors could give out fashion advice.

Solar panels are already becoming more and more popular.

Reuse, recycle and repair

In the future, we will build things to last and recycle anything that doesn't.

· People will have to pay to have rubbish removed — probably by robots.
· Bath and washing-up water will be recycled for watering the garden.
· There will be waste separation bins.
· Uneaten food could be turned into alternative fuel.
· Waste could be dumped in space!

Recycling plants, manned by robots, could be set up on other planets.

Robots

Robots will be part of normal life.

· Robots will do all the boring household chores.
· We'll have robot friends and pets.
· Robots will fight fires and crime.
· Robots will care for the growing elderly population.
· Miniature nanorobots will do things like sniffing out gas leaks.

Robots don't get bored or injured, so they're perfect for dull work.

Machines and gadgets

Machines and gadgets will be an even bigger part of our lives in the future.

- Televisions will get bigger.
- 3D televisions (without the silly glasses) will be commonplace.
- Cards with fingerprint or voice recognition will replace cash.
- Virtual worlds will let you ski or ride a horse without leaving home.

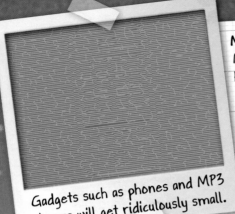
Gadgets such as phones and MP3 players will get ridiculously small.

Computers

Computers will continue to play an important role in everyone's lives.

- You will be able to operate computers by voice or even thought.
- Computers will be able to design and build even better computers.
- People will talk more on the internet than in person.
- Disposable computers will be developed.

Computers will continue to get faster and more powerful.

Personal flying suits will fly people when and where they want.

Travel

Virtual travel won't be enough — people will still want to get around.

- Cars that change into flying machines are already being made.
- Trains and aeroplanes will get bigger and faster.
- Airliners will fly without a pilot.
- Cars will become smaller and greener, with solar panels.
- Drivers will have implants to open car doors without a key.

Tourism

The growing population will have more time on their hands for holidays.

People will be able to enjoy virtual holidays at home.

Domed resorts will allow people to ski in deserts and sunbathe in snowy mountains.

People will be able to send video postcards containing sounds and moving images.

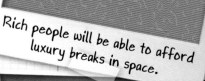

Rich people will be able to afford luxury breaks in space.

In the future people will travel into space for work, rest and play.

Other worlds

Space exploration and exploitation will increase with our crowded world.

· Colonies may be built on the Moon.

· The Moon and asteroids will be mined for gold, nickel and iron.

· Huge spaceships could pull asteroids closer to Earth for easier mining.

· Solar-powered satellites may harness the power of the Sun to solve the planet's energy crisis.

Schools

Like everything, schools in the future will be more high-tech.

· They will have robot guards.

· Schools will be open longer to fit in with busy parents.

· Each child will have a workstation with a computer and video console.

· Experts from around the world will give interactive video lessons.

School buildings will become

Healthcare

There will be huge changes to the way the sick and elderly are treated.

- More people will be treated at home with video-monitoring and robot carers.
- There will be robot doctors, nurses and surgeons.
- Nanorobots will enter the bloodstream to diagnose and cure illnesses.
- There will be a pill to cure almost anything — even the common cold.

Spectacles will disappear as laser technology is improved.

Amazing predictions

Here are a few remarkable ideas based on current trends.

- Probes will be able to record and store your memories and dreams.
- Machines will be developed to help people communicate telepathically.
- Scientists will solve hunger issues.
- Scientists will develop a biodegradable alternative to plastic.
- Human beings will land on Mars.

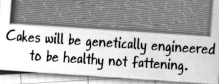

Cakes will be genetically engineered to be healthy not fattening.

Pop culture

- Avatar (2009) is a 3D movie set in the future.
- Dr Who is a British TV show about a mysterious 'time lord'.
- Star Trek is an American TV series about life on a starship.
- Back to the Future (1985) follows a teenager through time.
- Georges Méliès' A Trip to the Moon (1902) was the first-ever science-fiction movie.

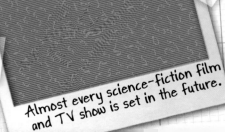

Almost every science-fiction film and TV show is set in the future.

"You will help us to colonize Clawmore," said Captain Savage. "One day, we will have filled the whole of space with Partek!"

"You can't make us obey you," I said.

"Perhaps," he replied. "But I can control your little friend."

He turned his blazing eyes on Plato, who stopped trembling at once.

"Stop it!" I demanded.

I could hear the other Partek almost giggling. Plato's eyes glazed over. I kneeled down beside him and put my hand on his back, but he didn't move or look at me.

"Plato?" I said. "Plato, you've got to fight it!"

Flecks of foam appeared on his lips and his body stiffened as if he had just seen a rabbit to chase.

"Take the humans to the Prison Bay,"

commanded Captain Savage.

Plato turned his eyes on me, and his lips curled back over his gums. A deep growl rumbled inside him. That was when I really started to feel scared. Plato loved me almost as much as he loved Grandpa Monty. If the Partek could turn him against me, they could do pretty much anything.

Plato started to walk forwards, stiff-legged. The other Partek joined him. Jamie and I were forced to back away. A door slid open behind us.

"If they try to escape, rip their throats out," Captain Savage told Plato.

We were taken down a maze of long corridors that led away from the centre of the ship. I was in a daze. I felt as if my whole world had turned upside down. I wanted to plead with them to release Plato. I wanted to attack Captain Savage.

Most of all, I wanted my dad to turn up and sort everything out. But I had to hold it together for Jamie.

"Do what they say for now," I said to him under my breath. "Don't worry, Jamie. I'm going to get you home, and that's a promise."

"I believe in you, Will," Jamie said. "I'm not scared."

I wished I could trust myself as much as he trusted me!

After stumbling along narrow, low corridors for ages, we arrived at a steel door. Plato stood and watched as the Partek opened it.

"Plato, mate, please snap out of it!" I cried, as the door slid open.

I don't think he even heard me. Clawed hands

pushed Jamie and me through the doorway, and then the door clanged shut. I heard about a dozen automatic bolts lock behind us. We were well and truly stuck there.

The Prison Bay was a huge space – about the size of four school sports halls and as tall as an aeroplane hangar.

"Will, look!" Jamie exclaimed.

It turned out that we weren't the only ones in the Prison Bay. There was a large huddle of people on the far side of the room. I reckon there were at least one hundred, and they all looked totally terrified. I walked towards them, and they backed away as if they were one huge animal.

"Stay back!" ordered a tall, dark-haired woman at the front.

"I'm not a Partek!" I said. "I'm a prisoner like you."

"Oh yeah?" she said. "Then how come you've arrived here so much later than everyone else? How do we know you're not the Partek playing some sort of sick joke?"

"Do I look like an overgrown cat?" I demanded. "The Partek and I have met before, and somehow they knew where I was. They came after me on purpose. My name's Will Solvit, and this is my... er...relative, Jamie."

I thought it was probably best not to tell them that Jamie was my great-great-great-grandson. That's the kind of thing that scrambles brains.

"I'm Violet," said the woman, who still looked a bit suspicious.

"Why did they abduct you?" I asked.

"I'm a military pilot," she said. "They teleported me and my plane up here. Not a fair fight, if you ask me."

"I don't think the Partek care about being fair," I said.

Before Violet could reply, something beeped in my pocket. It was my SurfM8 – and there was only one person who could be trying to contact me! I pulled the internet phone out and saw an IM from Zoe.

Invite Block Send File Save Display Pictures

To: Wilz

SingaporeSista: Will? Pls be there!

Wilz: I'm here, r u OK?

SingaporeSista: We r fine, where r u?

Wilz: Prison bay of Partek ship, headin 4 planet Clawmore. Partek using humans 2 colonize.

SingaporeSista: Jon sez is J OK?

Wilz: Yes, but the Partek r controlling Plato!

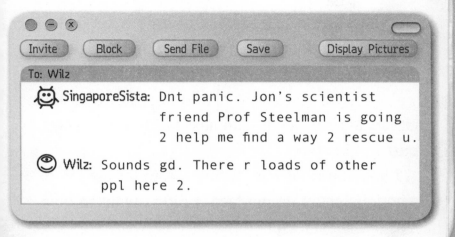

SingaporeSista: Dnt panic. Jon's scientist friend Prof Steelman is going 2 help me find a way 2 rescue u.

Wilz: Sounds gd. There r loads of other ppl here 2.

Suddenly I heard the bolts unlocking – the Partek were coming back!

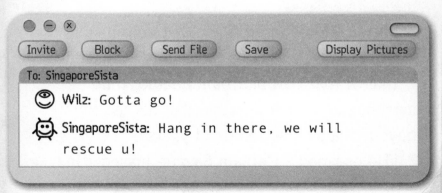

Wilz: Gotta go!

SingaporeSista: Hang in there, we will rescue u!

I shoved my SurfM8 back in my pocket just in time. The door slid open and Captain Savage stepped inside.

"I thought you might like to hear news of your father, Master Solvit," he said, with a mocking purr in his voice.

I just stared at him, trying not to let my emotions show on my face. I didn't want to give him the satisfaction.

"Henry Solvit was captured hundreds of years ago and taken to Clawmore," Captain Savage told me.

My mouth fell open. I couldn't help it.

"You mean, my dad's there now?" I asked.

I knew that Dad had built another time machine, so it was possible that he had time travelled across hundreds of years.

"He escaped," Captain Savage hissed. "But

Clawmore is in a dangerous part of space. Anything could have happened to him..."

He left the Prison Bay, smiling, and the door was bolted shut behind him.

"Are you OK?" asked Jamie.

His eyes were full of sympathy – I guess he thought it was bad news or something. But he didn't know my dad! I felt like dancing and shouting and singing. At last I had found out where Dad was taken after he left the Stone Age! It didn't matter that he had escaped – as long as I knew that he had once been on Clawmore, I could travel back in time and go and rescue him!

"What was that cat talking about?" Violet asked. "How could your dad have been captured hundreds of years ago? It's mental!"

I turned to her and took a deep breath.

"You are going to have to trust me, however

weird all this sounds," I said. "I'm a time traveller from your past."

"But you're only a kid!" Violet said.

Great, another prejudiced adult! Just what I needed.

"Yeah, I'm only a kid," I agreed. "But right now I might be our only chance of getting away from the Partek."

Violet stared at me in silence. I could tell that she was weighing me up, trying to decide whether or not to believe me. Finally I saw her shoulders relax.

"OK, Will Solvit, I'll trust you," she said. "So what's the plan?"

"As soon as I find out, you'll be the first to know," I promised her.

CHAPTER SEVEN
CLAWMORE

Suddenly the spaceship seemed to lurch, and my stomach felt a bit floaty.

"What was that?" cried Jamie.

"We've just hit super-lightspeed," Violet explained. "Wherever they're taking us, we're going to be there very soon."

There wasn't much time. I told Violet everything I had learned from Captain Savage about Clawmore, and she looked grim when she heard that we were supposed to colonize the planet.

"At least that means that the humans they have already taken must still be alive," she said.

The pet army rounded us up like sheep.

We were marched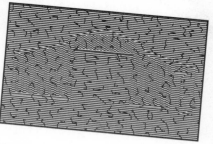
out of the Prison Bay
and down a ramp. We
had arrived at our new home.

Clawmore was a barren planet. It looked like
a wasteland. I turned around and stared in all
directions, but it was the same everywhere.
There were no trees, no streams and no hills.
There was no grass. The only things in sight
were hundreds of hypnotized pets, scores of
Partek and a large, metal building.

"What do you think is in there?" Jamie asked,
pointing at it.

"I reckon we're about to find out," said Violet.

She was right. We were marched towards the
building, which looked like a massive, metallic
barn. There was no door – just a big archway. I
guess they didn't need to worry about prisoners

escaping – there was nowhere to run to.

The barn was filled with people who looked up as we were pushed inside. They were all thin and pale. They were huddling together in groups, trying to protect each other against the bitter wind that blew across the planet's surface.

"We need food!" one of the men yelled at the Partek guards. "We're starving here!"

"You are fed once a week," hissed a Partek guard. "That's all you humans need."

The animals left and the people in our group went to join the other prisoners. Jamie and I looked at each other.

"So what's the plan, Will?" he asked.

I really wished I knew. I felt as if someone had dumped me in the middle of the Atlantic and I'd forgotten how to swim. But Jamie was relying on me – and I really didn't want to let him down.

Suddenly, Violet gave a yell from the other side of the barn.

"Did you say that your surname is Solvit?"

"Yes," I replied. "Why?"

She walked towards me, holding an envelope in her hand.

"Because this was on the floor over there," she said.

A wave of relief swept over me. I had never been happier to see one of those mysterious letters!

WHAT'S HAPPENING WHEN YOU HEAR WOOF ... SPLAT ... MEOW ... SPLAT? IT'S RAINING CATS AND DOGS!

THINGS ARE LOOKING SERIOUSLY DODGY, WILL. THIS COULD BE THE END OF THE HUMAN RACE.

THE PARTEK DON'T UNDERSTAND ANYTHING EXCEPT ATTACK AND BATTLE. YOU ARE GOING TO HAVE TO FIGHT FOR YOUR FREEDOM.

TAKE TO THE SKIES AND SHOW THE PARTEK THAT THEY CAN'T TREAT THE HUMAN RACE LIKE THIS!

"Take to the skies?" said Violet, who was reading the letter over my shoulder. "Some hope!"

Up until then I had forgotten that Morph was in my pocket. But suddenly I felt a sort of movement, like a phone vibrating. Morph was

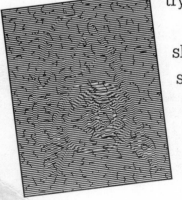

trying to tell me something.

"There is hope," I said slowly. "Violet, didn't you say that you're a pilot?"

80

"I can fly anything," Violet stated, her eyes flashing. "But if you think that we can steal one of those Partek spaceships, you can think again. We'd be torn to pieces before we could even get close."

"We won't need a Partek spaceship," I told her. "I just need your piloting skills."

"You've got them," said Violet, looking puzzled. "But how —"

I pulled the miniaturized Morph out of my pocket and rummaged in my backpack.

"Somewhere in here there's a memory chip for a ship," I said. "Morph's just going to have to find a way to make that a spaceship."

I had a lot of faith in Dad's invention. Morph certainly seemed to take control at times! Now I needed a mega-miracle. I found the memory chip and inserted it. Then I paused.

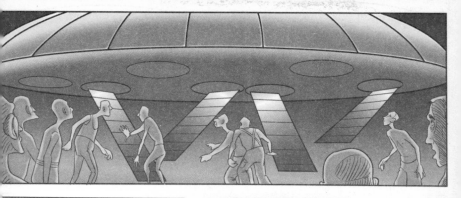

Violet was in shock.

Come on, you need to fly this thing!

STOP THEM!

"I'm not leaving Plato!" I shouted, seeing him and turning back.

"He's crazy!" Violet screamed.

I didn't know if she was talking about me or Plato, and I didn't care. I couldn't leave him behind. He leaped at my throat and I grabbed him. I lurched into Morph, holding the squirming dog and his snapping jaws well away from myself.

Morph retracted all the ramps, and the doors sealed shut. From inside, I could hear hundreds of Partek claws scratching on the metal.

"Jamie, get the rope out of my backpack!" I ordered, struggling to hold Plato still.

Jamie fumbled with my backpack zip. Violet slid into the control seat and adjusted the settings on the control panel.

"Here!" panted Jamie, handing me the rope.

I attached the rope to Plato's collar and then tied him to a metal loop in the corner. Morph had thought of everything!

Violet's fingers were flashing over the dials and buttons so fast that they were just blurs. There was a roar from the engines below us, and a tremor passed through the spaceship. Then we shot straight up into the sky as if someone was above us with a giant magnet.

"Yes!" I shouted, punching the air.

"WooHOO!" Jamie yelled. "Blast off!"

"We're not safe yet," said Violet. "Check out the radar."

There were dozens of flashing blips on the little radar screen, and several of them were already following us.

"Partek ships," said Violet. "Will, you and Jamie are going to have to take charge of the

weapons while I fly this thing."

"Awesome," I said, grinning at Jamie. "Come on, let's blast as many of those alien ships as we can find!"

I left Jamie at the controls and raced through the Morph-spaceship, checking that everyone was OK. Morph had created tons of seats, and all the escaped prisoners were busy strapping themselves in and chattering eagerly about seeing their families again. I just hoped they would get the chance!

I made my way back to the bridge. Jamie was checking out the weapons systems, and Violet was studying a holomap and cross-referencing it with the radar screen. It was all weirdly calm but I had a feeling it wouldn't be like that for long.

As we soared away from Clawmore, my SurfM8 beeped again. It was an IM from Zoe.

Invite   Block   Send File   Save   Display Pictures

To: Wilz

SingaporeSista: Will, what hppnd? U still OK?

Wilz: Hv escaped Partek! Morph now a spaceship!

SingaporeSista: Awesome! R u headin bk 2 Earth?

Wilz: Not as easy as tht. Tons of Partek ships here. Mega battle ahead.

SingaporeSista: U hv 2 get bk here. Earth in maj trouble. Partek invading BIG TIME.

Wilz: Oh no! R u safe?

SingaporeSista: No1 is safe. Darkness sweeping entire planet. Partek killin humans. World leaders captured. Armies in chaos!

Violet glanced at me. "Will, this is not the time to start playing computer games!"

"It's my friend Zoe on Earth," I said, feeling sick. "She says that the Partek have launched a massive invasion – it sounds as if they're killing anyone they can't capture! All the world leaders have been taken – there's no one to organize Earth's defences!"

"You're in touch with Earth?" gasped Violet. "That's incredible!"

"What's the use of us fighting the Partek here if they're destroying Earth?" Jamie cried.

"They'll be OK," said Violet. "Will, is your friend still in the same place where they picked you up?"

"I think so," I replied.

"Then she's really close to an entrance to a secret military bunker! It's on the other side of the hill from the public hideout caves. Here, I'll give her the coordinates."

She tapped the coordinates into my IM message.

"The password is kittycat," she said. "Tell her to lead as many people as she can down there. The bunker is hidden in the middle of the Earth, and it's crammed with battleships!"

I grabbed the SurfM8 and started to type as fast as I could.

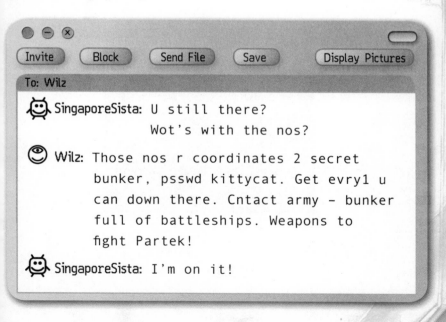

> **Invite**   **Block**   **Send File**   **Save**   **Display Pictures**
>
> To: Wilz
>
> 😺 SingaporeSista: U still there?
>   Wot's with the nos?
>
> 👁 Wilz: Those nos r coordinates 2 secret
>   bunker, psswd kittycat. Get evry1 u
>   can down there. Cntact army – bunker
>   full of battleships. Weapons to
>   fight Partek!
>
> 😺 SingaporeSista: I'm on it!

"Brilliant," I said, shoving my SurfM8 into my pocket. "We did it!"

"Not so fast!" said Violet, weaving the spaceship past a meteor storm and gritting her teeth. "The Earth troops still have to defeat the invaders, and that's not all."

"What do you mean?" I asked.

"I mean that we've got a fleet of Partek battleships on our tail!"

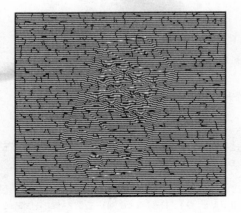

CHAPTER EIGHT
SPACE STEALTH!

"Strap yourselves in!" Violet yelled. "This is going to be a bit of a bumpy ride!"

Jamie and I jumped into the weapon-control seats and strapped ourselves in.

"Hold on to your stomachs!" Violet shouted.

She pulled up hard on the controls and we shot downwards in a massive loop-the-loop, coming up behind the Partek fleet.

"That was genius!" I whooped.

"Engaging cloaking device...now!" Violet stated.

We flew through the Partek fleet and I felt crackles of electric energy tingling through my veins.

"Why aren't they attacking us?" Jamie gasped.

"The cloaking device has hidden us from the Partek," Violet explained. "But it's only a matter of time before their technology strips our cloak off and reveals us. So we have to be ready to fire! In the meantime, I think I've got a little plan of my own..."

She weaved Morph among the Partek fleet at a speed that made me dizzy. One tiny wrong movement and we would be a splat on the side of a Partek battleship! Then she drew up beside one of the smaller ships on the edge of the fleet and turned to us.

"We are so ridiculously outnumbered it's not even funny," she said. "Surprise and stealth are the only advantages we have. I need one of you to do something impossible. I need you to capture that spaceship."

Jamie gawped at her.

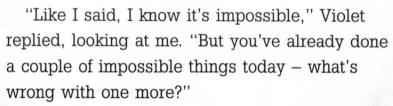

"But it's massive!" he said. "And full of Partek!"

"Like I said, I know it's impossible," Violet replied, looking at me. "But you've already done a couple of impossible things today – what's wrong with one more?"

"There is one chance," I said, delving into my backpack and pulling out the stun gun. "This will stun anything it hits. I could max out the settings so it's got the widest range...but we'll need to be really lucky."

"Let me do it," said Jamie, holding out his hand. "Mum always says I'm the luckiest kid she knows."

"No way!" I exclaimed.

"Will, I'm only a year younger than you!" Jamie pleaded. "And you go on Adventures all the time! I just want to help! I want to show that I'm a Solvit too!"

"That's decided then," said Violet, before I could say another word. "No time to have a debate about it. Jamie, get a spacesuit on and go."

I didn't like it, but I know how exciting it feels to face your first Adventure. I couldn't refuse to let Jamie experience that, however hard it was. I adjusted the stun gun settings while Jamie pulled on a silver spacesuit. It had an intercom built into the helmet, and we tested it to make sure that it worked. Then I handed him the weapon.

"Just point it and press that button there," I told him. "They'll go down like dominoes."

Jamie stepped into the airlock and went

through decompression. I saw the doors open, and glimpsed the large Partek battleship outside. Violet had pulled amazingly close.

"There should be a magnetic clamp inside the arm of your spacesuit," said Violet over the intercom.

"Er..." said Jamie.

I saw him peering down the sleeves of his spacesuit.

"Just point your right arm at the ship and press the blue button on your sleeve control pad," Violet instructed.

I had to hold onto my seat to stop myself from jumping up, finding a spacesuit and going out there to help him. Jamie pointed his arm at the Partek ship, and I saw a black clamp shoot over to the vessel and attach to the metal.

A thin, steel cord now linked Jamie to the ship.

He pulled himself across, slowly and steadily. What if one of the other ships spotted us? What if he pressed the wrong button and detached the cord? I realized that I was holding my breath.

Jamie reached the ship and clambered over to the nearest entrance hatch. He turned and waved at us.

"Wish me luck!" crackled his voice over the intercom.

"Good luck!" I called. "Leave the intercom open! And don't rush anything!"

"But keep it moving," said Violet, glaring at me. "We don't exactly have all the time in the world, kid."

The hatch opened and Jamie disappeared into it.

That was the worst five minutes of my life.

1st minute – I drummed my fingers on the

weapon firer until Violet got worried that I would set it off by accident and ordered me to stop.

2nd minute – I paced up and down, which made Plato go even more mental than he already was. Violet ordered me to sit down again.

3rd minute – We heard Jamie fire the stun gun over the intercom, followed by a whole bunch of yowling shrieks and more blasts of the gun.

4th minute – Silence. Jamie didn't answer us. I started to pull on a spacesuit. I was sweating in places I didn't know could sweat. Had I just sent my great-great-great-grandson to his death?

5th minute – There was another blast of the gun, and then we heard the clatter of Partek claws on metal. Jamie gave a yell and there was another series of gun blasts...and then silence. My insides turned to ice.

Then I saw Jamie's head pop out of the hatch

Very scary!

on the side of the Partek ship!

"All done," he said over the intercom, trying to sound casual.

"Cool," I said in a squeaky sort of voice.

We put a couple of the rescued prisoners onto the captured ship. They had orders to lock all the unconscious Partek in the Prison Bay and then fly the ship alongside Morph.

"Reckon you can go through all that again, Jamie?" asked Violet when he climbed back on board.

"Sure thing!" he said.

It was weird – he already looked older. He even looked taller! I wondered how much I had changed since I started Adventuring. Would Mum and Dad recognize me when I eventually found them?

Violet pulled up alongside another ship that

was on the outskirts of the fleet and Jamie repeated his performance. Once again I was wracked with panic for five minutes, and once again there was no need. He was a natural! I should have known. He was a Solvit, after all – he was born for Adventure!

We worked our way around the fleet, putting humans in charge of each ship we captured. By the time we reached the twentieth ship, Jamie had got his time down to three minutes and looked as if he'd been in a spacesuit all his life.

Jamie was about to attach himself to the twenty-first ship when Morph gave a little shudder and Violet groaned.

"That's it, guys!" she said. "They've broken through our cloaking device. They can see us! Man the guns!"

I couldn't help but laugh to myself when I

thought of Captain Savage hissing orders to his fleet – and then wondering why most of them weren't obeying! There were twenty-four ships in his fleet, and we had captured twenty of them.

"Incoming!" Violet yelled. "Strap in, guys!"

Jamie and I hurled ourselves into the weapon-control seats and fumbled to do up the straps. Morph's engines whined into overdrive and then the whole spaceship juddered as a rocket torpedo smashed into our side. Violet's fingers flashed over the controls and we were off, weaving through the friendly alien ships towards the main Partek battleship.

"Laser guns ready?" Violet shouted as a rocket torpedo flamed towards us. "Fire!"

Jamie and I fixed our sights on the rocket and pressed the weapons firer buttons. Streaks of laser fire speared through space and blew the rocket to smithereens!

Suddenly the holoscreen flickered – a message was coming through. I grinned when I saw Captain Savage's face.

"Hi, Whiskers!" I called, waving at him.

"You may have wiped out our communications, but you cannot wipe out our firepower!" he screeched.

I couldn't believe it. He still hadn't realized that we had control of the ships!

"He's got powerful shields," said Violet. "We're going to need one almighty blast to destroy his battleship!"

"Lucky we've got the Partek weapons then, isn't it?" I said.

"I will crush you under my claws like ants!" Captain Savage hissed. "You and your stupid planet!"

Earth fleet, prepare to fire!

I will wipe out every human!

FIRE!

The Partek ships blew to smithereens!

YES!

The Partek no longer had control over the animals!

Just one more thing left to do...

We sent the Partek back to Clawmore and loaded up the animals.

We headed back to Earth at super-light speed. As we entered Earth-space, we saw tons of space debris floating all around us.

"There's been one heck of a battle here!" said Violet. "Wow, this must have been awesome!"

She landed Morph beside the hidden underground bunker entrance, and let out a long breath.

"Of course, there is no way it could have been as awesome as ours," she added, grinning at us. "Thanks, you guys. Any time you want to join the military, I'd be honoured to have you on my team.''

''Thanks, Violet,'' I said. ''But right now all I want to do is find my friend!''

Morph opened a door and lowered a ramp to the ground. I raced outside with Jamie and Plato. I was really excited when I saw Zoe waiting at the foot of the ramp with Jon, Mandy and Sarah.

''Will!'' yelled Zoe. ''You're safe!''

Jamie raced up to his dad and started gabbling about the spaceships and the Partek and the stun gun. Jon's eyes nearly popped out of his head!

''It's been crazy here too!'' Zoe broke in when Jamie paused for breath. ''We told the army about the battleships underground, and they found pilots and coordinated this mind-blowingly massive attack on the Partek ships. You should have seen it, Will! The sky was lit up like a Christmas tree! There was so much fire-power that it was as if it was raining red and gold and blue!"

"The Partek skedaddled with their spiky tails between their legs," Jon added. "Now that they know Earth has a fleet of battleships to defend it, they've fled into deep space like the cowards they are."

"Good riddance," said Sarah, kneeling down beside Plato and patting him.

"That reminds me," I said, looking upwards. "We've brought a few Partek battleships with us to add to the Earth fleet...and there are hundreds of pets on board looking for good homes!"

Sarah's face lit up at the thought of having her own pet. She gave me a beaming smile as Violet walked down the ramp.

"The army's coordinating the spaceship landings," she said. "And I've volunteered to take control of all future defence against the Partek."

"You think they'll be back?" asked Jamie, his face falling.

"I'm certain of it," said Violet. "Those nasty little beasts will try to slither their way back here somehow, but next time we'll be ready for them."

"May I help?" asked Jamie, his cheeks reddening with excitement. "I'll do anything I can!"

Violet gave him a long, hard stare, and then reached out her hand.

"You were totally awesome today, Jamie," she said. "We couldn't have defeated the Partek without you. I'd be proud to have you as a member of the Earth Defence Force...or whatever we decide to call it."

Jamie shook her hand, looking as if he might pop with pride.

"Oh!" I exclaimed.

Everyone turned to stare at me. Now I could feel my cheeks growing hot.

"I just...I've got an idea for the name," I said.

"Fantastic idea, Will!" said Zoe, realizing what I was thinking.

"So what's the name?" Jon asked.

"The Alien Defence Unit," I said. "A.D.U. for short."

"A.D.U.," said Violet. "Yes, I like the sound of that. OK, the A.D.U. it is."

"Jamie Solvit, A.D.U.!" said Jamie, striking a heroic pose and holding out an ID card. "Paws in the air, Partek!"

"Jay, that's your library card," said Mandy, rolling her eyes. "Why are brothers always so embarrassing?"

Zoe grabbed my arm and drew me aside. Her

eyes were gleaming in exactly the same way they do when she's beaten me in a maths test.

"It's brilliant that your school project idea is going to come true," she said. "But now I've got someone I'd like you to meet."

She led me over to a man who was sitting on the grass nearby. His blond hair was sticking out at the sides, he had ink stains all over his forehead and his jacket was on inside out. I could see that he was drawing complicated diagrams in a small notebook, and he looked up as we reached him.

"Don't tell me," I said. "He's a professor."

"Will, this is Professor Adams," Zoe said. "He's a friend of Professor Steelman."

"Will Solvit, I presume," exclaimed Professor Adams, standing up, grasping my hand and pumping it up and down. "Spectacular to meet you! Read all about your father, of course. Wonderful man!"

"Professor Adams is going to convert the underground bunker where the battleships were stored into a giant recycling centre!" Zoe squeaked. "Isn't that mega-awesome? My idea is going to revolutionize the planet!"

"Brilliant!" I said. "Both our ideas are going to come true – how cool is that?"

"We should get more than an A plus," said Zoe, putting her hands on her hips. "We should get medals or something!"

"Yeah, well, I volunteer you for the job of explaining that to Mrs Jones," I said. "Talking of which, I have a feeling that this Adventure is about to come to an end."

I pointed at the space where our Morph-spaceship had been a few minutes before. Now the only thing that stood there was a full-sized time machine. Morph's door swung open.

"Think Morph's trying to tell us something?" Zoe said with a laugh.

We said goodbye to Professor Adams and walked towards Violet and my distant descendants.

"It's been amazing to meet you," said Jamie, shaking my hand. "That was a totally brilliant Adventure."

"Yeah, it was really bad," I said, remembering his slang.

Jamie laughed. "It just sounds wrong when you say it!"

"You did a mega-brave thing today," I told him in a low voice. "You know what? I wouldn't be surprised if you turned out to be a space Adventurer some day soon."

"What about us?" asked Sarah and Mandy in unison.

"I thought you weren't interested in Adventuring," I said.

"Yeah, well, Jamie had so much fun we might have to change our minds!" Mandy declared.

"Good luck with whatever you decide to do," I said. "Maybe I'll see you again sometime."

"I hope so," said Jon, shaking my hand. "My wife will be very sorry to hear that she missed meeting you."

"It's been totally awesome to meet you all," I said, "and a little bit weird!"

"Will, I think Morph's getting a bit restless," called Zoe from the doorway.

Morph was starting to glow. I raced over to join Zoe with Plato at my heels.

"Bye!" called Jon. "Have a safe journey!"

"Good luck with the A.D.U., Violet!" I called.

"We'll fight the Partek in your honour," she replied.

Then she stood very straight and stiff, and saluted me! It was a bit embarrassing, but it did feel pretty good!

"Will, come on!" Zoe demanded.

We gave a final wave and then closed the door. Immediately, Morph started to spin and shake. My teeth chattered against each other and my knees kept banging together.

"Morph, I w-wish you'd l-learn the c-concept of a s-smooth ride!" I yelled.

We were heading home!

"Who needs a roller-coaster when you could have a ride in Morph?" Zoe said, opening the door and peering out. "Yep, we're back in your bedroom. I can smell your stinky clothes pile from here."

I waited for my stomach to turn the right way up before I followed her out. I think Morph does it on purpose. Not even time travel needs to be that bumpy.

"Welcome back!" roared Grandpa Monty's voice. "Plato! Where have you been, you naughty boy?"

Grandpa was sitting on my bed, and Plato jumped up beside him.

Quack!

"He hitched a lift and nearly got himself turned into a cat," I said as Morph miniaturized. "Oh, and he travelled a few billion light years through space to a planet called Clawmore."

"He's always been far too easily influenced," said Grandpa, shaking his head. "I remember when he was a puppy we visited the local pond and he became convinced that he was a duck. Took me weeks to cure him of quacking."

Zoe gave a snort of laughter and I covered it up with a loud cough.

"Are you getting a cold, Isaac?" Grandpa demanded, drawing his bushy eyebrows into a frown.

"My name's Will, Grandpa," I reminded him.

"Here, have a chocolate-covered grasshopper.

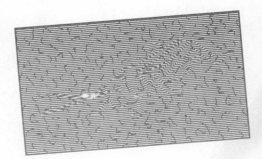

They're very good for warding off colds."

"Really?" I said, taking one of the spiky snacks.

"Well, have you ever heard a grasshopper sneeze?" he demanded.

In a weird way, he had a point. I popped the snack into my mouth and crunched on it, while Zoe pulled a disgusted face.

"It's quite nice," I said. "Kind of nutty."

"It's not the only nutty thing round here," said Zoe.

"So how long have we been gone?" I asked.

"Oh, only a few hours," said Grandpa. "It's nearly bedtime. Or is it breakfast time?"

"Bedtime," I said, looking out of the window at the night sky.

It felt great to look up at a sky that didn't have spaceships in it! Then I saw lights speeding up the drive. Zoe joined me at the window and groaned.

"That must be Mum come to collect me," she said. "Lucky we got back when we did! I wish she hadn't come yet, though – I wanted to talk to you about all the stuff that happened. Wasn't it an amazing Adventure?"

"It was dead cool," I said. "Message me later, yeah?"

Zoe nodded, said goodbye to Grandpa and went down to meet her mum.

"Now, I must go and brush my teeth," said Grandpa. "If I can find them, that is."

"Grandpa, you don't have false teeth," I said.

"Ah," he mused. "Well, that explains why I can't find them, doesn't it? Goodnight, Henry."

"Goodnight, Grandpa," I said with a grin.

I felt kind of relieved when the door closed

behind him and Plato. Grandpa Monty's awesome, but a ton of stuff had happened that day and I felt as if I really needed to sort it out in my head.

I picked up my notebook and looked at the cover where I had written The Diary and Clue Record of Will Solvit, Adventurer in fat red letters. I rummaged through the pile of pens on my desk until I found the big red marker. Then I changed the title as carefully as I could to:

THE DIARY
AND
CLUE RECORD
OF
WILL SOLVIT,
TIME TRAVELLING
ADVENTURER

Next I turned to the CLUES page. This was where I filled in all the facts I had discovered about my parents. Now I could add some more!

11. Dad was taken to Clawmore by the Partek, maybe after he left the Stone Age.
12. Dad escaped from Clawmore and the Partek don't know what happened to him.

I closed the book and stared into space. I knew all the clues off by heart now. When Mum and Dad first went missing, I thought that I'd be able to find them straight away. Obviously it wasn't going to be as easy as that, but every Adventure seemed to be bringing me closer to them.

A yawn took over my head and shoulders for about half a minute. My brain was foggy with tiredness. I picked up Grandpa Monty's old spy diary and flicked through it. He had had so many Adventures when he was younger – reading his diary was better than a novel any day!

Suddenly a picture on a page caught my eye and I stopped flicking. It was a (very) rough drawing of what looked a bit like a Partek, but I couldn't be certain that it wasn't a teapot. Grandpa's not exactly what you'd call a gifted artist. I read the diary entry to see if it explained the drawing.

Today marks the end of a highly successful mission, codename Operation Twinkle. At last I can record the true details of how I captured that notorious ring of diamond thieves, the Sahara Sparklers!

I knew that the thieves had hidden themselves away in Africa, but it was thanks to a tip from a disgruntled camel salesman that I tracked them to the Sahara desert.

Some agents would have rushed to arrest the crooks, but I knew better. I was sure that they must have hidden the diamonds somewhere in the desert – somewhere that only they knew. If I were to arrest them, I would have the satisfaction of seeing them behind bars, but I would never find the diamonds. No, I needed a cunning and subtle plan to outwit these robbers.

The idea came to me like a flash of genius. I would disguise myself! They would be suspicious of any human who came near them, but an animal was a different matter. After much thought (and no small amount of sewing) I settled into my new role as a lion!

It was a simple matter to make friends with the local lions and join their pride. I learned many things from those wonderful beasts while I lived among them. (The chief lioness taught me all I know about the preparation of raw meat.)

Each day I visited the camp of the Sahara Sparklers and listened to them talking. They did not see me, for I blended in with the sand so well. The thieves did not trust each other, and at last one of them returned to where they had hidden the diamonds, wanting to check that they had not been stolen.

That was all I was waiting for! With a roar of triumph I leaped from my hiding place and arrested them all. Yes, I was outnumbered seventeen to one, but I had the element of surprise! Not one of the Sahara Sparklers expected to be arrested by a lion, and that is how I locked them up and recovered the largest haul of diamonds the world has ever known!

Monty

"Brilliant!" I said.

I shut the diary and laughed out loud. I bet no one in the world has a grandfather like mine!

Another massive yawn overpowered me and I knew I couldn't fight it any longer — it was time for bed. I shuffled into the bathroom with my eyes closed and reached blindly for my electric toothbrush. It wasn't until I was ready to spit that I opened my eyes...and that's when I saw it.

A letter was taped to the bathroom mirror!

I didn't even wait to spit – I grabbed the letter and read it, forgetting all about feeling tired.

WHAT DO YOU GET WHEN YOU CROSS A NINJA WITH A VIKING?
A DEAD VIKING!

YOU DID A FANTASTIC JOB AGAINST THE PARTEK, WILL. YOUR NEXT ADVENTURE WON'T BE LONG FROM NOW, SO YOU'D BETTER BE PREPARED.

IT'LL TAKE PLACE IN ANCIENT JAPAN. FOR THE PEOPLE YOU'LL MEET, BATTLE IS A WAY OF LIFE.

P.S. WIPE YOUR CHIN.

I looked in the mirror – white trails of toothpaste were trickling down from the corners of my mouth. I spat and wiped my chin, my brain fizzing with questions. But if I knew anything about how these letters worked, one thing was certain. Wherever I ended up on my next Adventure, I was going to meet Japanese ninjas.

How cool was that!

OTHER BOOKS IN THE SERIES